Hiya! My name Thudd. Best robot friend of Drewd. Thudd know lots of stuff. How bug walk up wall. Why bubble break. How spider make web!

Drewd like to invent stuff. Thudd help! But sometime Thudd and Drewd make mistake. Invention plus mistake make adventure! Thudd and Drewd go on adventure now. Want to come? Turn page, please!

Get lost with
Andrew, Judy, and Thudd
in all their exciting adventures!

Andrew Lost on the Dog
Andrew Lost in the Bathroom

AND COMING SOON!
Andrew Lost in the Kitchen

ANDREW LOST

2
IN THE BATHROOM

BY J. C. GREENBURG

ILLUSTRATED
BY DEBBIE PALEN

A STEPPING STONE BOOK™

Random House 🏠 New York

www.randomhouse.com/kids
www.AndrewLost.com

Library of Congress Cataloging-in-Publication Data
Greenburg, J. C. (Judith C.)
In the bathroom / by J. C. Greenburg ; illustrated by Debbie Palen.
   p.   cm. — (Andrew Lost ; 2)
"A stepping stone book."
SUMMARY: After being shrunk by a shrinking machine and ending up
on a dog having a bubble bath, Andrew, his cousin Judy, and a tiny
robot try to survive encounters with insects, soapy bubbles, and
bathtub and toilet drains.
ISBN 0-375-81278-4 (trade) — ISBN 0-375-91278-9 (lib. bdg.)
[1. Size—Fiction. 2. Bathrooms—Fiction. 3. Bubbles—Fiction.
4. Adventures and adventurers—Fiction.]   I. Palen, Debbie, ill. II. Title.
PZ7.G82785 In 2002   [Fic]—dc21   2001048982

Printed in the United States of America
First Edition   20 19 18 17 16 15 14 13 12 11

CONTENTS

ANDREW'S WORLD

Andrew Dubble

Andrew is ten years old, but he's been inventing things since he was four! His newest invention is the Atom Sucker. It shrinks things by sucking the space out of their atoms.

Andrew wanted to shrink himself and write a report about ants. But at noon today Andrew had a little accident. Now he, his cousin Judy, and his robot, Thudd, are so small they could use the dot at the bottom of an exclamation point as a trampoline!

Judy Dubble

Judy is Andrew's thirteen-year-old cousin. She's pretty annoyed with Andrew for shrinking them. But Andrew shrank her parents' helicopter, too. If they can find it, she can fly them back to the Atom Sucker. But they have to hurry. In less than eight hours, the Atom Sucker will explode!

Thudd

Thudd is a little silver robot. The letters in his name stand for **T**he **H**andy **U**ltra-**D**igital **D**etective. He's Andrew's best friend.

Thudd has a super-computer brain. That means he knows just about everything. It also means he can never get wet. Unfortunately, he and Andrew and Judy are hanging off the ear of a dog that's about to get a bath!

Uncle Al

Andrew and Judy's uncle, is a top-secret scientist.

He invented Thudd! When Uncle Al made Thudd, he put a big purple button in the middle of Thudd's chest. Thudd is only supposed to press it in an emergency. He pressed it in the last book!

Harley

Harley is a basset hound. He belongs to Judy's next-door neighbor, but Judy is his best friend. Judy and Harley got even closer today. Judy was inside Harley's nose!

A few minutes ago, Harley dove into a smelly garbage bag. Now he's about to get a bath. . . .

Mrs. Scuttle

Mrs. Scuttle is Judy's next-door neighbor. Harley belongs to her. She is about to give Harley a scrubbing he won't forget. Andrew, Judy, and Thudd won't forget it, either!

1 A TERRIBLE FLAP

"Are we going to get out of this alive?" yelled Judy Dubble.

"Sure!" Andrew yelled back. But he was thinking, *If we get out of this alive, I'll never, ever do anything like this again, ever!*

Thanks to an accident with his newest invention, the Atom Sucker, Andrew was smaller than a flea's knee. And so were Andrew's cousin Judy and his robot buddy, Thudd. Now they were all dangling from a hair of a dog's floppy ear.

Ahwoooo!

The dog, Harley, was standing in a big white bathtub. Harley's owner, Mrs. Scuttle, was about to give him a bath! Water thundered out of the faucet. Hot steam curled into the air. Mrs. Scuttle's face was a huge, grumpy storm cloud above the tub.

Andrew thought about the two things that might save them. One was a cube of Umbubble in his back pocket. The other was the helicopter that had gotten shrunk, too. Andrew and Judy had been searching for it in the endless furry forest of dog hair. They hadn't found it yet.

Mrs. Scuttle wrapped her giant, squiddy fingers around Harley's collar.

"Get over here, mister!" she yelled. She yanked Harley to the front of the tub.

Woof!

Harley shook his head. His long brown ear flapped toward the roaring faucet.

meep . . . "Hang tight!" squeaked Thudd

from one of Andrew's shirt pockets.

Harley's ear hit the spray. Water drops sloshed over Andrew and Judy.

Andrew coughed and blew water out of his nose.

Thudd pinched his way up Andrew's shirt.

meep . . . "Oody okey-dokey?" Thudd squeaked as loudly as he could.

Judy pulled a strand of frizzy brown hair away from her eyes. "I'm smaller than the eye of a fly and hanging on to a soggy dog hair!" she yelled down. "What do you think?"

"I'm really sorry about this," Andrew called up to Judy. "I just wanted to write a great report on ants!"

"Dirty, dirty dog!" said Mrs. Scuttle, high above them. "This is what you get for rolling in garbage!"

A shower of pink dust rained down past Harley's ear. Andrew looked up to see that it

was pouring from a jar in Mrs. Scuttle's hand. The label on the jar read "htaB elbbuB."

Whoops! thought Andrew. *I'm reading it upside down!*

"Bubble bath!" he said.

"Ahhhh . . . *chooof!*" Judy sneezed. "I'm allergic to bubble bath!"

Bubble bath dusted Harley's head like pink snow. Harley shook his head. His ear flapped out like a furry magic carpet!

"Andrew!" screamed Judy. "I see something shiny inside Harley's ear! I think it's the helicopter!"

WHAPPPP! The ear smacked into the tub!

"Yaaarghhh!" Andrew screamed as he lost his grip on his dog hair. With one hand, he pushed Thudd into his shirt pocket. With the other, he reached for the little cube of Umbubble in his back pocket.

BUBBLE TROUBLE

"*Oof!*"

Andrew crash-landed onto something wet and rubbery. It was slippery as a fish! He started sliding fast down a shiny, curving wall of swirling colors—green and pink and red and purple.

When Andrew stopped sliding, he was upside down! His feet were caught in a drop of water at the bottom of a huge, clear globe.

"Where are we?" Andrew wondered.

meep . . . "Soap bubble!" said Thudd.

Andrew looked down.

Far below, mountains of suds rose from an ocean of water.

"Wowzers!" he said. "It's like we're hanging from a cloud!" Then Andrew realized there was something he *didn't* see.

"Where's Judy?" he asked.

meep . . . "Oody bounce off bubble," said Thudd.

"Oh no!" said Andrew. "And we can't even look for her because we're stuck here!"

meep . . . "Not for long," said Thudd. He pointed up. "See top of bubble?"

Andrew looked up through the bubble. The top was turning black!

meep . . . "Bubble skin thin, thin, thin!" said Thudd. "Must pile up million bubble skins to be thick as page of book. Bubble color tell how thick bubble is. Black mean bubble skin thin as can be. Ready to go 'Boom!'"

"Uh-oh," said Andrew. "I'd better get the Umbubble ready."

Andrew reached into his back pocket and pulled out one of his inventions. It was the size and shape of a piece of bubble gum. Bright blue letters on the white wrapper spelled UMBUBBLE.

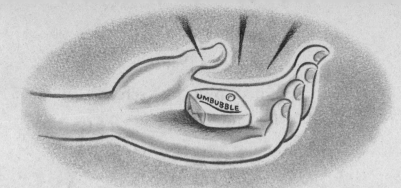

Andrew ripped off the wrapper and popped the little blue cube into his mouth.

"Tastes like grapes!" said Andrew, chewing. "The last one I made tasted kind of like—"

Just then, the rainbow soap bubble burst into a billion tiny drops!

"—MEATBAAALLLSSS!!!" Andrew yelled as he was blasted off the exploding bubble.

But a moment later, it felt as if a parachute had opened. He was floating!

"Neato mosquito!" said Andrew. "I wonder why we slowed down?"

meep . . . "Air filled with lotsa little molecules," said Thudd. "We so small, we bang into molecules! Make us fall slow. Like piece of dust! Look!"

Thudd pointed to his face screen.
"Cool!" said Andrew.

He watched shimmering soap-bubble blimps float past them. Twisting fingers of steam reached up from the water. Andrew and Thudd glided over the top of a glistening bubble mountain.

Then a drop of spray slammed into Andrew.

"Yaaaargh!"

3 UMBUBBLE TO THE RESCUE

Andrew stuck to the outside of the drop. It was like riding a giant water balloon!

Plop!

The drop crashed and dragged Andrew under the churning water near the faucet.

Thudd! thought Andrew as he held his breath and swam to the surface. Uncle Al had warned him that Thudd should never get wet!

As soon as Andrew popped into the steamy air, he pulled Thudd out of his pocket and held him above the water.

The buttons on Thudd's chest were blinking

red. They were supposed to be green!

meep . . . "Where sheep go to get haircut?" asked Thudd. There was a goofy smile on his face screen.

"What?" asked Andrew.

meep . . . "Baa baa shop!" said Thudd. "Hee hee!"

Then Thudd's eyes closed. *"Schnurm . . . schnurm . . . schnurm . . ."*

It sounded like Thudd was snoring!

"Thudd?" said Andrew.

He shook Thudd gently. Andrew was worried. Thudd had never told jokes before. And he'd never gone to sleep, either.

The Umbubble in Andrew's mouth was nice and soft now. Andrew started blowing a clear blue bubble.

When the Umbubble was twice as big as he was, Andrew stopped blowing. The Umbubble floated gently on the water.

There was a little hole in the Umbubble

where Andrew had been blowing. Andrew
pushed himself through it. The walls of the
Umbubble were thin and rubbery and a little
sticky. They stretched tightly around Andrew
and kept the water out, then snapped shut behind him.

*I'd better keep my legs in the water so I can
paddle around the tub,* thought Andrew. He

pushed his legs back through the Umbubble.

As soon as the Umbubble sealed up tight again, Andrew started blowing on Thudd, trying to dry him off.

Thudd's eyes opened.

"Are you all right, Thudd?" asked Andrew.

meep . . . "Wet! Wet! Wet, Drewd!" Thudd whimpered. "Dizzy, too."

Andrew stuck Thudd to the wall of the Umbubble to dry.

"Drewd seen Oody?" Thudd asked.

"Not yet," said Andrew. "Did you see where she landed after she bounced off the bubble?"

meep . . . "Oody fall near there!" said Thudd. He pointed to a mountain of bubbles between the faucet and one of Harley's towering legs.

"She's so small," said Andrew. "Do you think we can see her?"

meep . . . "Thudd use Goggle Scope!"

The Goggle Scope was a clear, flat mask that let Thudd see things in different ways. It sat on top of his head when he wasn't using it.

Thudd pressed the Goggle Scope button on his chest, and the Goggle Scope flipped down over his face screen. Thudd pressed another button to set the Goggle Scope to "telescope." This made faraway things look near.

Andrew kicked through the choppy bathtub sea toward the bubble mountain. Blobs

FLUMP

of soapsuds rained down as Mrs. Scuttle scrubbed Harley.

Ahwoooo! Harley howled.

"Down, mister!" yelled Mrs. Scuttle.

Harley's paw smacked the water.

"Whoa!" Andrew yelled as a swirl of water caught the Umbubble and dragged it toward the bubble mountain. An avalanche of bubbles began to tumble down from its top!

The bubble mountain collapsed, and a dark, craggy island came crashing through it!

4 SKELETON CREW

The huge mound loomed high above them. It was brown and covered with deep, dark caves and shaggy ridges. And it was headed straight for the Umbubble!

"It looks like an asteroid!" said Andrew as he paddled quickly away from it.

meep . . . "Sponge!" said Thudd.

"Jeepers creepers!" said Andrew. "It doesn't *look* like a sponge. The ones we use to wash the dishes are all bright colors and shaped like rectangles!"

meep . . . "Drewd use fake sponges," said

Thudd. "Fake sponges made in factory. Real sponge here. Real sponge is skeleton of sponge animal that live in sea. Look!"

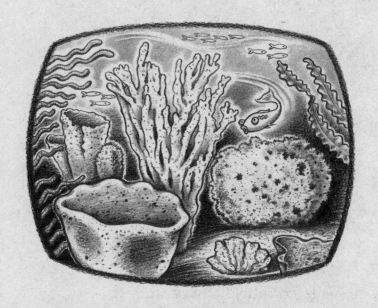

The sponge was getting closer.

"That's a real weird skeleton," said Andrew as he paddled faster. "I thought skeletons had to be hard."

meep . . . "Sponge animal got squishy skeleton," said Thudd.

Andrew looked into the sponge's dark, spooky caves. "What are all those holes?" he asked.

meep . . . "Sponge animal not got mouth," said Thudd. "Sponge animal suck water through holes. Eat little stuff that float in water."

Sccreeeek!

Andrew looked up. Mrs. Scuttle was turning the knob on the faucet. Niagara Falls turned into a trickle and stopped!

meep . . . "Drewd!" Thudd cried. He pointed toward the top of the sponge. "Look! Oody!"

Andrew strained his eyes. "I guess she's too small for me to see without the Goggle Scope," he said.

Thudd pressed another button on his chest. A beam of light popped out of a little hole at the top of Thudd's head. At the end of the beam, Andrew saw a picture of Judy standing near the top of the sponge. It was like watching television!

Judy had taken off her blue denim jacket. She was waving it frantically.

Then something crept up behind Judy. At first all they could see was a shiny black head and long antennas. Its jaws looked like an enormous lobster claw!

"An ant!" yelled Andrew. His eyes widened. "Oh no! It's coming toward Judy!"

The ant tapped its antennas on the sponge behind Judy. But Judy didn't seem to see it.

meep . . . "Scout ant," said Thudd. "Use antennas to find food and water. Eyes not see much."

"Let's hope it can't see Judy!" said Andrew.

meep . . . "Smell and taste stuff with antennas. Then scout make smell trail for other ants to follow."

The ant stopped tapping the sponge. It was suddenly very still. Andrew held his breath. Then the ant raised its antennas high.

Andrew and Thudd watched in horror as the ant tapped Judy on the head with an antenna!

Judy turned. Andrew was too far away to hear her scream, but he could see the scream on her face! Her feet scrambled! It looked like she slipped! Then she cartwheeled off the sponge and disappeared into a cloud of steam!

GETTING ANT-SY

Andrew paddled frantically around the sponge, but he couldn't find Judy anywhere.

"Where *is* she?" he asked.

Then Andrew felt a tug on his foot. He looked down to see frizzy brown seaweed floating below. It was Judy's hair!

"Judy!" Andrew yelled.

Judy was stuck underneath the Umbubble!

"Grab on to my legs!" he yelled.

The seaweed nodded.

Andrew yanked his legs into the Umbubble.

Snap!! The top half of Judy came in with them.

"Welcome to the Umbubble!" said Andrew. He helped her the rest of the way inside. The Umbubble sealed up behind her.

Judy took a deep breath. "Ah . . . *choof*!"

meep . . . "Bless oo!" said Thudd.

"Thanks!" said Judy, pushing her hair away from her face. "That stupid bubble bath got up my nose. But it's better than being on a disgusting sponge with yucky ant antennas in my hair!"

Judy flopped back against the Umbubble.

Thudd pushed his Goggle Scope button. The Goggle Scope flipped back up to the top of his head.

meep . . . "How do you know if water friendly?" asked Thudd. "It waves! Hee hee!"

Judy leaned over to look at Thudd.

"I've never heard Thudd say anything silly," said Judy. "And how come his buttons are yellow?" she asked.

Andrew explained how he and Thudd had fallen from a soap bubble into the bath. He also told Judy about Thudd's first joke and the snoozing.

"Thudd isn't supposed to get wet," Andrew

said. "I hope he's okay. But at least his buttons are yellow now. It's better than red."

Judy tickled the bottoms of Thudd's rubbery feet. He always liked that.

meep . . . "Thunkoo!" said Thudd. His face screen turned pink as a wide smile stretched across it.

"Thudd seems okay now," said Judy. "Did Uncle Al call while I was gone?"

"Noop," said Thudd.

More than an hour ago, Thudd had pressed the big purple button in the middle of his chest. It was supposed to contact Uncle Al in case of emergency.

"What time is it?" asked Judy.

meep . . . "2:15," said Thudd. "Five hours and forty-six minutes left."

Judy frowned. They needed to get back to the Atom Sucker in Judy's backyard by 8:01. If they didn't set the Atom Sucker to UNSHRINK before then, it would get hot enough to blow up! And then they'd be stuck at microscopic size forever.

Judy leaned back and folded her arms across her chest. "I'm pretty sure I saw the helicopter in Harley's ear," she said. "If we can get to it, I can fly us back to the Atom Sucker. There's an open window above the toilet. But how can we get up to Harley's ear?"

They looked up at Harley's head, high as a cloud above them.

Andrew leaned back against the Umbubble, which was rocking gently on the waves.

"You know," he said, "I think I have some waterproof matches in one of my pockets somewhere." Andrew patted his shirt.

Judy rolled her eyes. "Andrew, you've probably got a kitchen stove in your pockets somewhere!"

Andrew smiled as he poked his hands into his pockets. "Hot air rises," he said. "If we could heat the air in the Umbubble, maybe we could get the Umbubble to rise up to Harley's ear!"

"Noop! Noop! Noop!" said Thudd. "No fire inside! Fire eat up oxygen in air! Drewd and Oody not breathe!"

Judy sat up straight and stared through the Umbubble. "Look!" she said, pointing at the bottom of the sponge. "There's that ant again!"

They watched it creep along the sponge.

"What if the ant walks across the water to get us?" asked Judy. "Remember those water bugs we saw in the stream behind Uncle Al's house?"

Andrew nodded. "Water bugs were scampering around on the water like it was a sheet of plastic," he said.

meep . . . "Water molecules hug tight, tight, tight!" said Thudd. "Top of water like thin, thin skin. Small thing can walk on water skin. Look!"

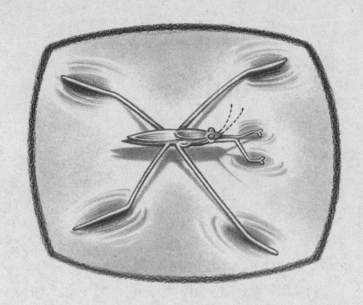

Judy gave a little shiver. "Start paddling, Andrew!" she said. "That ant could walk over here any second!"

"Noop!" said Thudd. "Cuz soap break water skin. Bug sink!"

Suddenly Thudd's big purple button started to blink.

GLOORP!

meep . . . "Uncle Al!" said Thudd.

"Finally!" said Judy. "Uncle Al will know what to do!"

Thudd's purple button popped open and a beam of purple light flashed out.

A see-through, slightly purple Uncle Al floated outside of the Umbubble at the end of the beam. Uncle Al's shaggy hair made him look as if he had just pulled a shirt over his head. The shirt he was wearing had a picture of a tarantula spider on it. Andrew and Judy had given it to him for his birthday.

Uncle Al's face crinkled into a smile. "Hey there!" he said.

"Uncle Al, thank goodness you're here," said Judy. "You see, we've got this little problem—"

"I'm away from my laboratory at the moment," continued the slightly purple Uncle Al.

"Huh?" said Andrew.

"Oh no!" said Judy. "It's not Uncle Al, it's some kind of answering machine!"

"Your message has reached my Hologram Helper," said Uncle Al. "If you're calling to have a friendly chat, please press one. If you have discovered life on another planet, please press two. If you want to complain about smells coming from my laboratory, please press three. If this is a purple-button emergency, I will contact you in person as soon as possible."

Uncle Al waved. "Good-bye! Have fun! Think big!"

The Uncle Al hologram faded and disappeared.

Judy kicked her foot against the Umbubble.

Boing!

"Great!" she said. "Where's Uncle Al?"

"Don't kick the Umbubble, Judy," said Andrew. "Uncle Al got our signal. He'll call us back." But Andrew's voice was softer than usual.

"Ahwoooo!" howled Harley high above them.

"I'm going to wash that dirty doggie face whether you like it or not!" said Mrs. Scuttle gruffly.

A black shape dived toward the Umbubble. It was Harley's nose!

"Cheese Louise!" cried Judy. "Not again! I refuse to drown in dog snot twice in one day!"

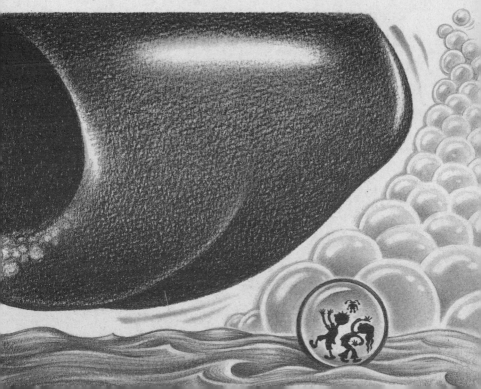

The nose swooped so low they could look into the midnight darkness of Harley's nostrils! Just two hours ago, they had been inside them! Then the nose lurched away.

They heard Harley's paws scratching at the front of the tub, and then a strange sound.

gloorp . . .

"What was that?" Judy asked.

The Umbubble started moving in a circle.

gloorp . . . *gloorp* . . .

"Bad dog!" boomed Mrs. Scuttle. "You pulled the plug!"

"Oh no!" Judy moaned. "Harley opened the drain!"

The Umbubble was picking up speed! The water was carrying the Umbubble toward the drain!

gloorp! . . . gloorp! . . .

Andrew stuck his legs back through the Umbubble and started kicking as hard as he could. But the current was too strong!

gloorp . . . gloorp . . . GLOORP!

The front of the bathtub was getting closer. They were about to get sucked down the drain!

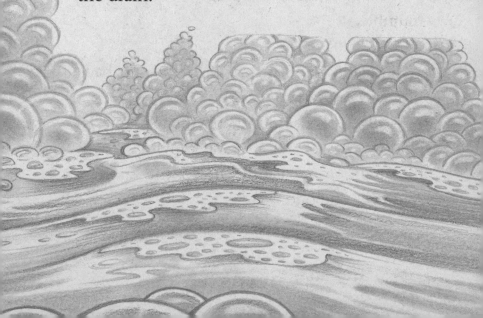

A DISTANT RELATIVE

Sploooosh!

Mrs. Scuttle's hand plunged into the suds in front of the Umbubble.

"Now, where is that plug?" they heard her mumble.

GLOORP!

"Maybe Mrs. Scuttle will get the plug back in," said Andrew nervously.

Judy looked around the tub. Sponge Island was beside them. It was moving toward the drain, too. "Paddle us to the sponge, Andrew!" she said.

"What about the ant?" Andrew asked.

"Either we get ourselves onto that sponge or we go down the drain!" Judy said. "Here, I'll help."

She pushed her legs through the Umbubble and started kicking.

But the current held the Umbubble like a train on a track. They couldn't get to the sponge! The drain was getting closer and closer.

Ahwooooo!

Water splashed and soap bubbles popped as Harley bounded out of the tub. The Umbubble bounced and spun in the rough water.

"You come back here, mister!" screamed Mrs. Scuttle. She rushed after Harley—and left the drain open!

Out of the corner of his eye, Andrew caught a glimpse of something big coming up behind the sponge. It looked like a smooth white iceberg!

"Holy moly!" said Andrew. "Look at that!"

meep . . . "Bar of soap!" said Thudd.

"It's as big as the *Titanic*!" said Judy.

The soap bashed into the sponge. The sponge smashed into the Umbubble!

Thump!

"*Oof!*" hollered Andrew and Judy as they slammed back against the wall of the Umbubble.

The next thing they knew, Andrew and

Judy were looking into the yawning mouth of a huge, spooky cave. The Umbubble was stuck to the bottom of the sponge!

Almost all the water had drained out of the bathtub, but the sponge was still sliding slowly toward the front.

Suddenly Thudd's purple button started blinking. The button popped open. Out came the purple beam. Outside the Umbubble, at the edge of the sponge cave, a purple, transparent Uncle Al was waving at them.

"Unkie!" said Thudd.

"Uncle Al, is it really you?" Andrew asked.

"It had better be," said Judy.

Uncle Al laughed. "That sounds like Judy. And is that Thudd and Andrew, too?"

Andrew and Judy looked at each other, confused.

"It's us, Uncle Al," said Andrew. "Can't you see us?"

"Oh! I guess I should explain!" said Uncle

Al. "I can hear you but I can't see you. Not with this model of the Hologram Helper. I'm still working on it. Are you okay? What's the purple-button emergency?"

"Well," said Andrew. "The first thing is, we're really small—"

"Of course you're small!" said Uncle Al. "You're only ten years old! You'll grow! I don't think that's a purple-button emergency, Andrew."

Judy rolled her eyes. "Uncle Al, we're smaller than flyspecks! We've been up a dog's nose! We got dragged off by a flea! We've been attacked by eyelash mites! Now we're inside this rubbery Umbubble thing and stuck under a sponge that's sliding toward the drain in Mrs. Scuttle's bathtub!"

Uncle Al's eyebrows went up. "Ah! Well, that's a different story!"

Judy went on. "We've got to get back to the Atom Sucker. That's the gizmo Andrew invented that shrunk us. It's in my backyard."

"And we've got to get back by 8:01 tonight," Andrew added.

"What happens at 8:01?" asked Uncle Al.

"The Atom Sucker might kind of . . . blow up," said Andrew.

"And we'll be stuck like this forever!" said Judy.

"Humpty Dumpty on a Ritz cracker!" exclaimed Uncle Al. "This *is* a purple-button emergency."

Suddenly, the left half of Uncle Al disappeared.

"I hope this doesn't mean you're leaving, Uncle Al," said Judy.

"What do you mean?" asked Uncle Al.

"Half of you isn't there!" said Judy.

Uncle Al's voice sounded far away. "There must be a problem with Thudd's antennas. I may not be able to stay long."

The right half of Uncle Al started to fade.

"Come back!" said Andrew. "I've got to tell you about Thudd!"

But Uncle Al turned as clear as a raindrop and disappeared completely.

8 SLIME CITY

"Great!" said Judy. "*Now* what do we do?"

All the water was out of the tub. But the sponge was still shoving the Umbubble slowly through a slush of dirty gray soap scum and dog hair.

Outside the tub, Harley was howling.

"You get your tail over here!" Mrs. Scuttle hollered. "I'm not finished with you yet!"

Suddenly the Umbubble came to a jolting stop.

"The sponge must have hit the front of the tub," said Judy.

"Uh-oh," said Andrew. They were hanging over an enormous dark hole. It looked as if it went down forever. "We're hanging over the drain!" he said.

Thudd crept down to Andrew's knee to get a look.

Sticking to the sides of the drain were all the things that get washed away in bathtubs—eyelashes and nose hairs and nose goo and pieces of toenails and skin flakes and old scabs and all kinds of dirt. And all of that was covered with a thick coat of oozy slime.

"Euuw!" said Judy. She yanked her legs inside the Umbubble.

"Slime gravy!" said Andrew. He yanked his legs in, too. "Everything is grosser when it's slimy!"

meep . . . "Slime alive!" said Thudd. "Look at—"

Just then Thudd's purple button started blinking again. It snapped open and beamed out the Uncle Al hologram. This time, Uncle Al was inside the drain!

Judy chuckled. "Uncle Al, do you know you're up to your belt buckle in slime?"

"Good golly, Miss Molly!" said Uncle Al. "I wish I could see it! Slime is amazing stuff! It's made by bacteria, which some people call germs. Bacteria cover themselves with slime blankets to protect themselves from stuff that can hurt them! Bacteria build whole cities out of slime! They even send messages to each other through slime! Thudd, show Andrew and Judy a slime city."

meep . . . "Look!" said Thudd.

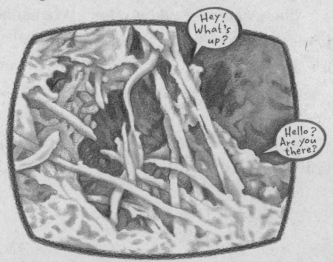

"That's interesting, Uncle Al," said Judy. "But we have more important things to worry about right now."

"Oops!" said Uncle Al. "I'm sorry. I didn't mean to get carried away! Andrew, you were about to tell me something when we were cut off last time. I think I know what it is. Did Thudd get wet?"

"How did you know?" said Andrew.

Uncle Al nodded. "That's why we were disconnected," he said. "The soapy water removed the protective coating from Thudd's antennas. Has Thudd been snoozing?"

"Yes," said Andrew.

Uncle Al scratched his chin. "What about jokes? Is Thudd telling jokes?" he asked.

"Uh-huh," Andrew said. "I'm awfully worried about him."

"It sounds like Thudd's thought chips are soggy," said Uncle Al. "Thudd hasn't told any elephant jokes, has he?"

"No," said Andrew.

"Good," said Uncle Al. "Telling elephant jokes would be much more serious."

Uncle Al looked thoughtful. "This is important," he said. "You must keep Thudd from getting wet again. And you need to stop him from rusting. Rubbing him with something greasy would do the trick. Something like—butter!"

Judy spoke up. "Uncle Al, how in the world are we supposed to get butter? We're the size of pinpoints and we're stuck to the bottom of a sponge!"

"An unusual problem," said Uncle Al, nodding. "But solving unusual problems is what we Dubbles do best!"

"Could you come help us?" asked Andrew.

"I'm leaving right now," said Uncle Al. "But I'm all the way up at the Arctic Circle," he added.

Uncle Al was starting to fade away.

"Wait!" yelled Judy.

"I'm sorry!" called Uncle Al. "I can't hear you! But remember this: When you've got an unusual problem, look at everything in an unusual way! You have everything you need . . . in your . . . heads . . . and . . . in . . . your . . . pockets. . . ."

Uncle Al disappeared. And in his place was—

"The ant!" cried Judy.

The huge black head, antennas waggling, was coming up from the drain. Its clawed feet reached out and pawed the bottom of the sponge—right next to the Umbubble!

9 A TANGLED WEB

The ant bent its head toward them. They stared up at its giant clipper jaws.

"It could bite right through the Um-bubble!" said Judy.

Ahwooo! Harley yowled.

"Back into the tub, mister!" Mrs. Scuttle yelled. Her voice sounded close.

The ant tapped the Umbubble with its hairy black antennas.

meep . . . "Ant antennas smell us!" said Thudd. "Can tell if we taste good!"

The ant's jaws were spreading open!

Andrew and Judy were frozen in terror when they heard the flap of the shower curtain against the tub.

"What's that on the ceiling?" they heard Mrs. Scuttle say. "I just got rid of one yesterday!"

Suddenly the sponge was moving. Water oozed out of it!

The ant wagged its enormous head, then skittered off the sponge and back into the drain.

"Look!" said Andrew.

A curved pink wall appeared next to the Umbubble. It was so high they couldn't see the top. It was covered with ridges that looked like the rows of a plowed field.

meep . . . "Thumb!" said Thudd. He pointed to the strange ridges. "Fingerprints!"

A waterfall tumbled over the Umbubble

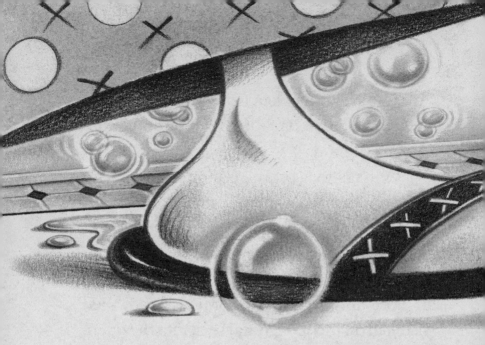

as Mrs. Scuttle squeezed the sponge. Soap bubbles popped up everywhere!

Andrew and Judy watched the tub getting farther away. The sponge, with the Umbubble stuck to it, was going up!

"*Sit,* Harley!" came Mrs. Scuttle's rough voice. "I'm going to get rid of that thing once and for all!"

They saw one of Mrs. Scuttle's humongous feet in a flip-flop. She had stepped onto the edge of the tub.

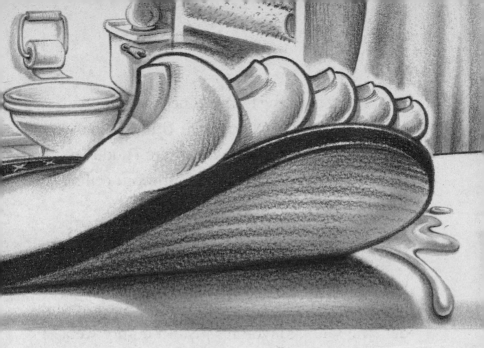

"What is she going to—" Judy started to say.

"I'll *get* you!" yelled Mrs. Scuttle.

Suddenly they were hurtling toward Mrs. Scuttle's ceiling!

"*EEEIIIIIY!*" Mrs. Scuttle howled.

There was a tremendous thump, like a mountain falling into a valley. Then there was a softer thump. It was the sponge falling back into the tub. But the Umbubble was swinging like a circus trapeze from the ceiling!

"We're dangling from a rope!" said Andrew.

meep . . . "Spider web!" said Thudd. "Look!"

Andrew and Judy looked where Thudd was pointing. The corner of the bathroom ceiling was a jumble of crisscrossed spider webs.

"Cheese Louise!" said Judy. "We just escaped getting gobbled by an ant. Now we could end up as a spider snack!"

Andrew looked around. "I don't see a spider," he said. "Maybe it's just an empty web. Maybe Mrs. Scuttle clobbered the spider."

Judy and Andrew heard more thumping sounds below. Through the open shower curtain, they could see Mrs. Scuttle sitting on the bathroom floor, pounding her fists on the tiles. Harley was trying to lick her face.

"She must have slipped off the edge of the tub when she threw the sponge," said Judy.

"Uh-oh," said Andrew, looking at the tub below. "We're hanging right above the drain.

If this spider web breaks, it's slime city for us."

meep . . . "Spider silk strong, strong, strong!" said Thudd.

"I know," said Judy. "My parents led a tour to an island near Australia. The spiders made webs so strong that people made fishnets out of them."

"Wowzers!" said Andrew. "I'll bet I can use spider silk in one of my—"

"Andrew!" yelled Judy. She pointed to a fold in the shower curtain. It was twitching. . . .

HOLD YOUR BREATH!

While they watched, a dinosaur-sized spider crept out from behind the shower curtain fold. It looked like a monster cement mixer. Its body was yellow-brown and its head was bullet-shaped and furry. Its legs were long and hairy with brown and yellow stripes.

The spider let go of the shower curtain and swung away on a thread attached to its rear end.

When the spider stopped swinging, it was hanging right below the Umbubble!

meep . . . "Spider make dragline," said

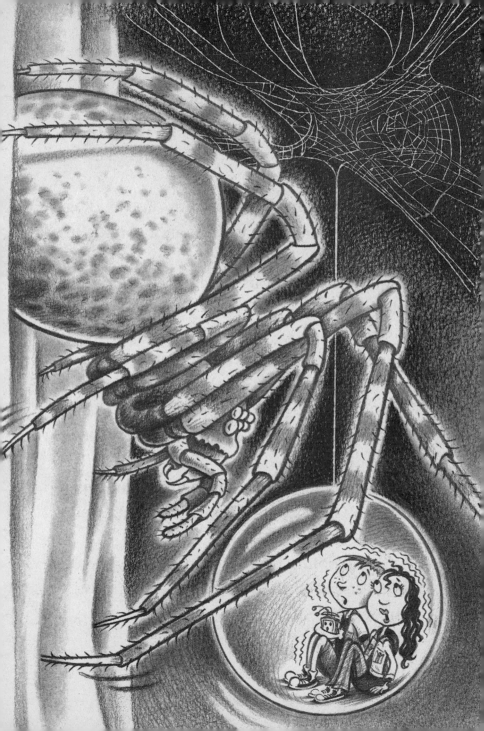

Thudd. "Special silk thread for escape. Spider swing away when sponge attack. Look!" Thudd pointed toward the ceiling. "End of dragline stuck to web."

The spider started to scurry up the dragline. They could see its furry face coming up toward them. Two fangs stuck out at the bottom. At the top of its head were two rows of black eyes.

meep . . . "Spider got eight eyes," said Thudd. "But spider not see much. See hairs on spider? Hairs feel web move. Tell spider what caught in web. Tell spider where to find it. If spider touch our thread, spider feel us move. Feel us talk!"

Now the spider was right across from them on its dragline. They could see the hairy underside of it.

Judy pointed to finger-shaped nozzles on the rear end of the spider. "What are those?" she whispered.

meep . . . "That where spider silk come from," said Thudd softly.

The spider moved up past them on its dragline. Then it paused. It reached out with two of its long, hairy yellow-and-brown legs and pawed the air. Then the spider crossed over to the thread the Umbubble was hanging from!

Andrew looked at Judy. He put his finger up to his lips. Judy nodded.

They stayed as still as they could. They barely breathed.

Andrew looked over at Thudd. His eyes were closing. *Oh no!* thought Andrew. *He's going to start snoring!*

"*Schnurm* . . ." Thudd snored. It was so loud, the Umbubble trembled!

"*Schnurm* . . . *schnurm* . . . *schnurm* . . .*"

Andrew looked at Judy. Judy looked at Andrew. Her eyes were round and her mouth was saying a silent "Eeek!"

The spider stopped in its tracks. It turned and started scrambling down toward the Umbubble.

It was no use being quiet anymore.

"We've got to get out of here!" Andrew said.

"If we bounce up and down, maybe we can get the Umbubble to pull away from the spider silk," said Judy. She started to bounce.

Andrew looked down. "Even if we end up in the drain, it's better than being eaten by a spider," he said. He started bouncing, too.

meep . . . "Whazzit? What happen?" said Thudd, waking up.

"Uh, nothing, Thudd," said Andrew. He didn't want to make Thudd feel bad about attracting the spider's attention. "But the spider is coming at us, so we're trying to get loose from this thread."

The spider's hairy face was just outside the Umbubble. It was like a huge cat staring into a tiny fishbowl.

"Eeeeyyyiiiiiii!" came a yell from below. Andrew and Judy turned to see a wall of tree trunks speeding toward them!

THIS TRIP STINKS!

"Mrs. Scuttle's got a broom!" Judy screamed.

The broom smacked the Umbubble, smashed through the web, and hit the bathroom wall. *Whaaap!*

The Umbubble whizzed through the air like a tiny baseball.

Then, in a few seconds, the Umbubble began to slow down. It drifted gently through the air.

"Whew!" said Judy. "At first it was like being in a speeding car. Now it's like a hot-air balloon ride!"

They were getting close to the edge of the shower curtain.

Andrew leaned forward. "What are those spots on the shower curtain?" he asked. "They look like little black islands."

"It's just dirt," said Judy.

meep . . . "Fungus," said Thudd.

Little currents of air dragged the Um-bubble closer to the shower curtain. The black spots began to look like something else.

"It looks like a forest of black trees," said Judy.

meep . . . "Fungus not plant," said Thudd.

"Fungus special kind of living thing. Watch out! Stay way from fungus!"

"Oh, come on," said Judy. "A mushroom is a fungus. There's nothing dangerous about a fungus."

meep . . . "Fungus roots turn Drewd and Oody into juice and suck them up," said Thudd. "That how fungus eat!"

"Super yucky!" said Andrew.

The Umbubble touched the thin black branches at the top of the fungus.

"Cheese Louise!" said Judy. "I am not going to get turned into people juice by a stupid fungus!"

Judy shoved her legs through the Umbubble and gave her biggest soccer kick. The Umbubble bobbled away from the fungus.

"Whew!" sighed Judy. "Now that we're small, it seems like everything is alive—even specks on shower curtains."

They were drifting over the edge of the

tub and past the shower curtain.

"Super duper pooper-scooper!" said Andrew. "We're away from the bathtub! And there's the window over the toilet! It's open! Now we just have to get into Harley's ear and find the helicopter."

Mrs. Scuttle was on her feet again, standing by the sink. She had Harley by the collar and was wiping his ears with a washcloth.

Judy looked toward the window.

"Wait a minute!" she said. "Maybe we don't need the helicopter! If we could find a way to steer the Umbubble . . . Hmmm. Uncle Al said to look at things in unusual ways. And he said we have everything we need in our pockets. Andrew, you've got more pockets than a herd of kangaroos. You check your pockets and I'll check mine."

Andrew was still looking through his pockets when Judy pulled a pen out of one of hers.

"That's interesting," she said.

She opened the pen and pulled out the ink cartridge. She poked the hollow tube of the pen through the wall of the Umbubble. Then she started to blow through it.

The Umbubble bobbled forward! She moved the tube down and the Umbubble went up. When she moved the tube left, the Umbubble went right.

"YES!" Andrew cheered. "Now we can steer the Umbubble. We can float ourselves back to the Atom Sucker!"

"Yup," Judy said, smiling. "I think this will work."

As Judy blew, they floated slowly away from the tub. They watched Mrs. Scuttle pull a pink towel from a shelf piled high with towels. The whole pile tumbled to the floor!

"This is the worst day of my life!" moaned Mrs. Scuttle.

Harley ran over to the laundry basket near the bathroom door and started to shake himself dry. A hurricane of water drops flew up into the air!

meep . . . "Get hit by water drop, Um-bubble crash!" said Thudd. "Like when Drewd get sunk before."

"I'm trying to get us away," said Judy, puffing hard into the tube.

"Stop that!" Mrs. Scuttle yelled at Harley.

She shook out the towel and threw it over him.

"HARLEY!" screamed Mrs. Scuttle. "Don't you *dare*! *NOOO!*"

A gusty breeze from the tossed towel

caught the Umbubble and sent it tumbling toward the ground.

"Eek! Errrgghh! Ooof!" cried Thudd and Andrew and Judy as the Umbubble crashed on the hard white tile of the bathroom floor.

"I feel like a tossed salad," Judy said. She sniffed the air. "Peuuuw! What's that smell?"

12 OOPS!

meep . . . "Poop!" said Thudd. He pointed to a monster brown mound beside the Umbubble.

"Cheese Louise!" said Judy. "It's the Himalayas of doo-doo! The Mount Everest of poop!"

"Now you've done it, mister!" yelled Mrs. Scuttle. "Pooping on the floor! *Bad* dog! I've a mind to send you to the animal shelter. You won't be seeing much of that *Judy* girl you like so much!"

"Oh no!" said Judy. "I *love* Harley! We've got to rescue him!"

"I guess we've got to rescue ourselves first," Andrew said.

Suddenly the light in the bathroom seemed to flicker. Andrew looked up. At first he thought the ceiling was falling, but then he realized what was happening.

"Uh-oh!" he said. "Mrs. Scuttle's got toilet paper and she's coming at us!"

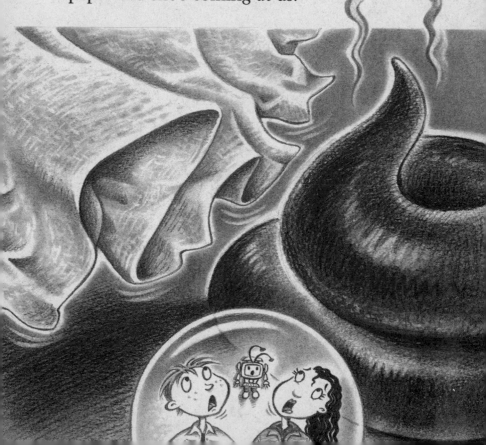

In the next second, the toilet paper plopped down over them and swooped them—and the poop mountain—off the ground. The sticky Umbubble was stuck to the bottom of the toilet paper. They were going up, up, up! Andrew watched the tiles of the bathroom floor get farther and farther away.

Clunk!

"You know what that sound is?" asked Judy.

"Um, no," said Andrew.

"It's the lid of the toilet clunking against the tank," said Judy. "Mrs. Scuttle is getting ready to flush us!"

"Uh-oh!" said Andrew.

meep . . . "If Umbubble get flushed, end up in big cement tank deep, deep underground," said Thudd.

"I *know*," said Judy. "I used to make plumbing for my dollhouses when I was a little kid."

Now they were right above the toilet bowl! Mrs. Scuttle's hand was reaching for the handle of the toilet!

"Cheese Louise!" said Judy. "This is the worst thing ever!"

"At least we're inside the Umbubble," said Andrew. "We've got plenty of air, so we won't drown if we get flushed."

"It's not *if* we get flushed," said Judy. "We're *going* to get flushed. In about one second!" She pulled the empty pen tube out of the wall of the Umbubble and put it back in her pocket. The Umbubble sealed itself up. "We don't want any leaks!" she said.

Crrrunk! Mrs. Scuttle pulled down the handle of the toilet!

A whirlpool of water churned below.

meep . . . "What is red and white on outside, gray on inside?" asked Thudd. "Campbell's Cream of Elephant soup! Hee hee!"

Oh no! thought Andrew, remembering

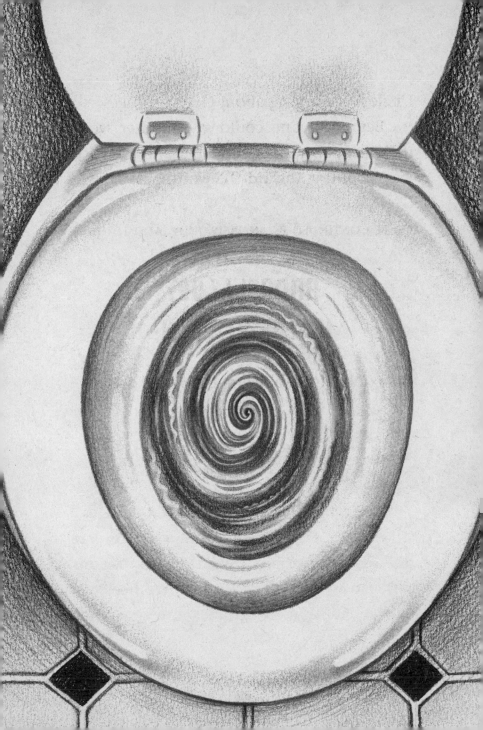

Uncle Al's warning about elephant jokes.

Before anyone could say another word, the toilet paper, the Umbubble, and the poop were zooming toward the whirlpool below!

TO BE CONTINUED IN ANDREW, JUDY, AND THUDD'S NEXT EXCITING ADVENTURE!

ANDREW LOST
IN THE KITCHEN!

In stores November 26, 2002

TRUE STUFF

Thudd knows a lot, and what Thudd says is true! Thudd wanted to say more about what happened in the bathroom, but he was getting a little rusty. This is what he wanted to tell you:

• The skin of a bubble is a soap-and-water sandwich—soap on the outside and water on the inside. Bubbles break because the water part of the bubble dries out. People have kept bubbles "alive" for almost a year. How long can *you* keep a bubble alive?

• When you chew gum, you're chewing sticky sap from trees!

• Bacteria reproduce by splitting in two. They can split every hour. So if you start with one bacterium, in an hour you'll have two bacteria. After two hours, you'll have four. Guess how many you'll have in 24 hours? (Find the answer at the bottom of the page.)

• Spiders don't have teeth, so they can't chew their food. Instead, spiders squirt juices into their prey that turn its insides into goo. Spiders eat by sucking out the goo!

• There are spiders as big as a human hand! Some of them catch and eat small lizards and birds. These spiders bark!

• The biggest living thing on earth may be the humongous fungus in Oregon. It's larger than Rhode Island and almost as big as Delaware!

• Bacteria and fungi (say "FUN-guy") recycle everything that dies and all kinds of waste. Without them, the earth would be piled high with poop!

You can find out more about bubbles and bacteria—and many *other* things!—at www.AndrewLost.com.

16 million! Use a calculator to prove it. But most of them die! (Lucky for us!)

WHERE TO FIND MORE TRUE STUFF

There's weird stuff all around you! You may not be able to see it, but you can read about it in these books:

• *MicroAliens: Dazzling Journeys with an Electron Microscope* by Howard Tomb and Dennis Kunkel (New York: Farrar, Straus and Giroux, 1993)

• *Hidden Worlds: Looking Through a Scientist's Microscope* by Stephen Kramer, with photographs by Dennis Kunkel (Boston: Houghton Mifflin, 2001)

Would you like to blow a bubble as big as you are? Want to find out who kept a bubble going for almost a year? Check out:

• *The Unbelievable Bubble Book* by John Cassidy with David Stein (Palo Alto, CA: Klutz, 1995)

If you don't believe soap and water are

interesting, take a look at these books:

• *Soap Bubble Magic* by Seymour Simon (New York: William Morrow & Co., 1985)

• *Soap Science: A Science Book Bubbling with 36 Experiments* by J. L. Bell (Toronto: Kids Can Press, 1993)

Do you want to find out more about insects and spiders? Find these books:

• *Micro Monsters* by Christopher Maynard (New York: DK Publishing, 1999)

• *Megabugs* by Miranda MacQuitty with Laurence Mound (New York: Barnes & Noble Books, 1995)

You can learn a lot about bugs from this book—and it's funny, too!

• *Ugly Bugs* by Nick Arnold (New York: Scholastic, 1998)

Turn the page
for a sneak peek at
Andrew, Judy, and Thudd's
next adventure—

ANDREW LOST
IN THE KITCHEN!

Available November 26, 2002

TOILET BOWLING

When you wake up in the morning, thought Andrew, *you never think about getting flushed down the toilet!*

Andrew, his older cousin Judy, and Andrew's robot, Thudd, were stuck inside the Umbubble. The Umbubble was whirling round and round a toilet bowl. Their neighbor Mrs. Scuttle had just flushed the toilet!

"Cheese Louise!" said Judy. "It's like we're at the top of a water tornado!"

The Umbubble picked up speed, and the light above them faded away. It was as dark as a bad dream!

GLOOGGGUHHH! The toilet roared.

meep . . . "Hope Umbubble not leak,"

Thudd squeaked into the darkness.

"If this thing springs a leak," Judy said, "I'm using Andrew's head to plug it!"

Then the Umbubble slammed to a stop.

"Yergh!" said Andrew.

"Oof!" said Judy.

"Eek!" said Thudd.

"I think we're stuck," said Andrew.

Suddenly the big purple button in Thudd's middle started blinking! The button popped open and a beam of purple light shot out.

At the end of the beam floated an image of Uncle Al.

"Uncle Al is back!" said Andrew.

Uncle Al was smiling. But Andrew could tell he was worried.

"Hey there!" Uncle Al said. "I'm on my way! Where are you guys now?"

"We got flushed down the toilet!" said Andrew. "Now we're stuck in the drainpipe."

"Good golly, Miss Molly!" said Uncle Al. "This is serious. But I have an idea. The pipe that leaves the toilet connects to all the other pipes in the house. You should be able to find a pipe that leads up to a sink."

"I'll get my mini-flashlight," said Andrew. He unhooked a little flashlight from his belt and turned it on.

The Umbubble was surrounded by mounds of gooey jelly! Stringy things were floating in the goo. And little blobs were squirming through it!

"We're in some kind of jam!" said Andrew.

"A seaweed-and-blob jam!" Judy said.

Uncle Al nodded. "Sounds like slime," he said. "The seaweedy stuff is fungus and the blobs are—"

Suddenly Uncle Al started disappearing. First his feet disappeared, then his legs. Finally, all that was left was his shaggy hair.

"Uncle Al!" Judy yelled. "Don't go!"

But it was too late. Uncle Al's hair disappeared, too!

ANDREW LOST—AGAIN!

Andrew, Judy, and Thudd are lost in a deep, dark, creature-filled cave!

ANDREW LOST

14

WITH THE BATS

BY J. C. GREENBURG

Thanks to another invention mishap, Andrew, Judy, and Thudd are the size of bugs. Being small is a big problem when they get lost in a cave full of bats! Will Andrew and his friends find their way out?

"Andrew Lost books are gross and disgusting. That's why we like them."—*The Washington Post*

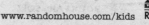